Dinosaurs Don't Dance: A Lesson on Authenticity

The Developing Dino Tale Series

Identifiers: ISBN: 979-8-9881377-1-9 (paperback)

QUANTITY PURCHASES: Schools, companies, clubs and other organizations may qualify for special terms when purchasing a quantity order. Contact jollyfoxbooks@gmail.com for information.

Written by Elyse Fox
Illustrated by Garrett Fox
Book design by Elyse Fox, Garrett Fox

jollyfoxbooks.com

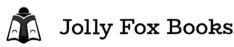 Jolly Fox Books

Dinosaurs Don't Dance
A Lesson on Authenticity

A Developing Dino Tale

Written and Illustrated by
Elyse and Garrett Fox

In a valley lush and green
Rupert did delight,
With spiky plates along his back,
Armored like a knight.

Bright gold scales adorned his frame,
But he stood apart
With his love for dancing to
The beat within his heart.

Rupert loved to shake a leg -
Twirl and spin all day.
His heart was filled with passion
With every graceful sway.

Rupert moved with charm and poise.
T'was a sight so grand.
Other dinos didn't dance,
So would they understand?

Dinos liked to stomp and roar,
Playing all the same.
But Rupert knew that dancing
Was where his pleasure came.

Rupert spied his dino crew
Playing with much glee.
Stomping, roaring as they should,
He joined cheerfully.

Stomps that shook the muddy earth,
Forceful and mighty.
Roars filling the big blue sky -
What a sight to see!

With his stomping, roaring friends
Rupert tapped and swayed.
In a twirl his dance began
Sweeping him away!

As he danced his friends all stared,
Pointed, mocked and teased,
Saying words unkind and mean,
Laughing on their knees.

"Dinosaurs don't dance!" one yelled.
"That's just how we're bred.
All we do is stomp and roar.
What's inside your head?!"

"You'll never be a dinosaur.
You just won't fit in."
Judging what Rupert loved -
They got under his skin.

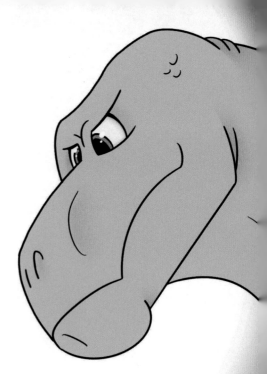

"I am too a dinosaur!"
Rupert did exclaim.
So he stopped his happy bops,
Inside feeling shame.

Rupert knew deep in his heart
Dancing wasn't wrong.
But being happy wasn't worth
A chance to not belong.

So Rupert roared with his friends,
Hiding what he knew.
Stomping wouldn't bring him joy.
It did not feel true.

Rupert's tail then slumped and dragged
As he walked away.
Longing deep within his heart,
Would he dance today?

Later he heard Daisy's voice
Softly from the trees,
"Rupert hey, what's got you down?
Won't you tell me, please?"

Rupert sighed, then said aloud,
"They said we don't dance.
Now that's all I think about,
Like I'm in a trance!"

"All they do is stomp and roar,
Forced to play one way.
Everything has stayed the same
Each and every day."

"Such a silly thing to speak,
Dinosaurs don't dance.
They're just stuck in their old ways.
Step up, take a chance!"

"True friends will embrace your quirks
Even if offbeat.
They'll be fond of your hobbies,
Loving you complete."

"Now some news I'll share with you -
Singing is my trait.
Melodies just fill my soul!
Why hide how I'm great?"

"Instead I choose to be with
Friends who can relate.
And together we've become
Part of something great!"

"See, I think your dances rule,
Special and unique.
True to who you <u>really</u> are -
A talented green geek!"

Then as Daisy's voice rang out
Rupert itched to move.
Her mousy song got him into
A funky dancing groove.

Through all the day they had fun,
So much song and dance.
Rupert's moves now feeling free,
Three cheers this second chance!

By both sharing their passions,
They learned something new.
When you hide bits of your heart,
You're never being you.

Laughter, smiles and merriment,
The crew saw the scene.
Joyful moments by two friends,
Recalling they were mean.

But instead of judging them
New thoughts came to be.
Fancied joining in their fun,
Setting their hearts free.

We would stomp and roar before,
Blinded how to play.
We should walk the path that puts
Our hearts on display.

One came up and said real proud,
"Stomping I would dread.
I'd much rather spend my time
upside down instead!"

"I would stomp and roar all day
Feeling like a dud.
But inside I truly love
Playing in the mud!"

"Stomping, roaring, nothing else.
Surely I had doubts.
Now to share that I love
To curl my tail and bounce!"

One last dino cleared its throat
Staring at the floor.
"Corny sure, but truly I
...LOVE TO STOMP AND ROAR!"

All their hearts could now play free
Accepting everyone.
Earlier they'd stomp and roar,
Now it was <u>true</u> fun."

Time flew by while spirits sang.
Many hours passed.
When you're out there having fun
Time can go by fast!

Knowing now that true friends would
Welcome weird and strange,
Loving all what makes you tick.
Don't you ever change!

Let this be a lesson to
All who feel real down.
There are those who accept you -
Now you can be found.